As is natural, some "pot-shots" miss their mark. Some are—
again, natural enough—merely platitudes stood on their heads
so as to give the appearance of paradoxes. But others are
witty, unexpected, charming, wry—most enjoyable.
                                        —*Clifton Fadiman*

I MAY NOT BE TOTALLY PERFECT, BUT PARTS OF ME ARE EXCELLENT

© 1973

And Other
BRILLIANT THOUGHTS

By
ASHLEIGH BRILLIANT

Woodbridge Press Publishing Company
Santa Barbara, California 93111

Published by

Woodbridge Press Publishing Company
Post Office Box 6189
Santa Barbara, California 93111

Published simultaneously in the United States and Canada

Printed in the United States of America

Library of Congress Cataloging in Publication Data

Brilliant, Ashleigh, 1933-
   I may not be totally perfect, but parts of me are
excellent, and other brilliant thoughts.

   1. Epigrams. I. Title.
PN6281.B68   818'.5'402   79-10052
ISBN 0-912800-66-6
ISBN 0-912800-67-4

3

Dedication

*Part of this Book
is Dedicated to You,
and the Rest
to You-Know-Who.*

Ashleigh
Brilliant

TRY TO BE
THE BEST OF
WHATEVER YOU ARE,

EVEN IF
WHAT YOU ARE
IS
NO GOOD.

BEST
OF THE
WORST

In This Book . . .

I MAY NOT BE
TOTALLY PERFECT,
BUT PARTS OF ME
ARE EXCELLENT.

Ashleigh
Brilliant

How Do I Do?

Ashleigh Brilliant is my real name. I was born (in England) in the same year that Franklin Roosevelt and Adolf Hitler began to rule the World (1933), and have never quite recovered from the shock of losing both of them when I was only twelve years old (1945).

The following purely malicious rumors about me are all true:

1. I was once arrested in Madrid for wearing shorts (1952).

2. I gave a public speech in Red Square, Moscow, on the subject of Human Rights, and was subsequently expelled from Russia (1959).

3. I was the first person ever to use the official University of California Free Speech Platform at Berkeley (April 12, 1962).

4. On April 7, 1967, I was publicly designated a "hippie" by the San Francisco *Examiner*.

5. In May, 1969, I was arrested in Cape Town, South Africa, for riding in a car with the sign, "ATTENTION CAR THIEVES—THIS CAR IS ALREADY STOLEN."

6. I was the subject of a major Free Speech demonstration at the University of Oregon (Eugene, February 3, 1965) at which twelve members of the faculty stood on the steps of the English department building, and gave a public reading of an "obscene" poem.

7. It took me fifteen years, instead of the usual five, to become a U.S. citizen, (August 26, 1969), because I was accused of having an immoral relationship with a woman whom I had produced as a witness to my good character.

8. The British headmaster who had once caned me at school for criticizing the teaching methods of one of my teachers, later applied to become my business agent (1971).

9. I am guilty of holding degrees from three Universities, and became a Doctor of Philosophy by writing an incredibly scholarly work on the *Social Effects of the Automobile in Southern California During the Nineteen-Twenties* (Berkeley, 1964).

10. I am also the author of the notorious *Haight-Ashbury Songbook* ("Songs of Love and Haight"), which Herb Caen of the San Francisco *Chronicle* denounced as "good clean fun," and which was (no doubt) a major corrupting influence in the celebrated San Francisco "Summer of Love" (1967).

11. My career as a professional teacher of history has been more or less awash ever since I taught for two round-the-world semester voyages on the famous "Floating University," then administered by Chapman College (1965-67).

12. My art work was considered so unacceptable for display in the Arts and Crafts Show of Santa Barbara, California, that a special law was passed to keep it out (1976).

13. As a candidate for the Santa Barbara City Council (1977), I conducted my entire campaign in song (and lost).

14. Patty Hearst once wrote to me and said, "You must be out of your mind, but I love it!!!"

So now you know something about me. Obviously, I am some kind of professional trouble-maker, working both inside and outside the system. Or, if you want to be more kind, you can call me a pioneer. This book is the result of a particular kind of pioneering effort which I have been making, with increasing seriousness, for most of my life—an attempt to say some important things (ideas which, of course, have all been expressed in some fashion before) in a new and perhaps better way. As you can see from my name, it requires no immodesty for me to call them *Brilliant Thoughts*. They have already been published under various other names, such as *Pot Shots*, and in a variety of media, but this is their first appearance under this name, and in book form.

How I Invented This Game

I would like to be able to say that from the very beginning I knew exactly what I was doing and had a careful plan, of which you see here the final and perfect result. The truth, of course, is nothing of the sort. It all began with miscellaneous bits of thinking which I jotted down from time to time on miscellaneous bits of paper, and, not knowing what else to do with them, I simply stashed them away.

When at last I couldn't stand keeping them to myself any longer, I began reading them aloud to groups of friends, calling them one-line poems, or "Unpoemed Titles." To emphasize that each line was a completely separate piece, I would pause between lines to make some kind of sounds on whatever sound-making instrument happened to be handy, and would encourage my audience to do the same.

Many people urged me to illustrate and publish these works, but I hesitated, seeking a form which would continue to put space between them. At last I hit on the idea of publishing them as *postcards,* which solved the problem nicely, and had several additional advantages. (1) The postcard form combined openness with intimacy, just as my writings were attempting to do. (2) It had a practical purpose: unlike an ordinary book, my "one-page books" could not only be *read*, but also *used*. (3) It was easy to become one's own publisher; and, assuming that the messages had commercial appeal (which, much to my surprise, soon became evident), the whole thing had tremendous business potential. My first cards were published in San Francisco in 1967, and, if you count each card as a separate work, I am surely by now one of the world's all-time best-selling authors.

At some early point in this undertaking, it occurred to me that I was in the process of creating something so new and different that it hardly fitted into any established category. In one sense, it was an entirely new form of literature. Of course, there have always been proverbs, epigrams, and "grafitti" of various kinds. But very few writers in our language (apart from the pitiable hacks of the greeting card industry) have ever devoted themselves to creating an extended series of such works; far fewer have ever asked or expected to be taken seriously as writers; and none, so far as I know, has ever attempted to publish each brief utterance as a separate copyrighted literary work. With all deference to Chairman Mao and other authors whose quotations derive from longer works, it seemed that I was becoming the world's first writer of self-contained ready-made quotations.

In another sense, the significance of my work seemed to be at least as much scientific and sociological as literary. I was creating a new kind of instantaneous communication. The entire message was right there, on one side of one piece of paper, and could be read in a flash. My postcards were what Marshall McLuhan might one day call the last gasp of Gutenburg—a bridge between the dying technology of print and the new age of electronic communication.

Convinced of the importance of what I was doing, I began to develop a set of rules and guidelines to give it distinct shape and character. The most important of these was *brevity*. No *Brilliant Thought* must ever exceed a maximum of seventeen words. Why seventeen? First, because, at the time I made the decision, I found that the longest line I had yet published had seventeen words. Secondly, I was perhaps influenced by knowing that the Japanese *Haiku* form of poetry is limited to exactly seventeen syllables (not words).

A second major rule was *universality*. One object of the game, I decided, was to reach as many minds, over as much of the world, and as far into the future, as possible. Therefore the words must be simple, easily understood, and easily translated. Their effect must not in any way depend upon rhyme, rhythm, puns, or any other kind of conventional word-play. For the same reason, all topical, local, and even cultural allusions must be avoided. On the other hand, in order to reach everybody, I must be free to discuss every conceivable topic, including those not necessarily considered very pleasant and those not commonly publicly aired at all. In particular, I wanted to say the kinds of things which most of us feel, but many of us find very difficult to express.

With so limited a format, the challenge was to pack the most possible insight, amusement, intelligence, and feeling into the fewest possible words. And, since "word-play" was ruled out, there must be free rein for "meaning-play," in such forms as irony, ambiguity, subtlety, audacity, paradox, and crazy logic.

The casual reader of these works is not usually aware of the high degree of discipline upon which they are based; but that, of course, is as it should be, and is itself the result of another of my rules: a *Brilliant Thought* should be expressed in something approximating ordinary colloquial speech. It should sound like something that somebody might say. But there is also the vital rule of *originality*, which demands that, to the best of my knowledge, it is substantially different from anything anybody ever actually *has* said before.

But what about the pictures? You will already have gathered that it is the words with which I am primarily concerned. And one of the intentional features of this work is that the words are not dependent on the "art" for their impact, and can be fully appreciated without any graphic accompaniment. This makes it very different from the conventional "panel cartoon," which usually consists of an illustration and a caption, which are both necessary for a full understanding and enjoyment of the work. In illustrating the words, I try to avoid depicting specific situations. I provide instead a sort of oblique commentary, leaving it to you, the reader, to find your own particular applications for the words. For the same reason, I have avoided the temptation to create a comic-strip-like "cast of characters," although you will find a bearded figure appearing occasionally, who remotely resembles me.

Am I Playing This Game, Or Is The Game Playing Me?

So, what happens when you spend years of your life putting pieces of your mind on thousands of cards, and sending them out to make their own way in the world? It was such a new game that I had no idea what to expect. I hoped vaguely to discover if there was anybody like me out there. I also wanted to see how far a person like me could go in a world like this, simply by being myself, and letting everybody know it.

The results have in many ways been very strange. For one thing, I soon discovered that *Everybody* out there is somehow like me, or at least they all *seem* to think they are, although often their only evidence is just one *Brilliant Thought* which they may have seen on a card or in a newspaper somewhere. People often write to me saying things like "I never knew anybody else had these thoughts and feelings. Now I don't feel so alone any more."

Another thing that happens is that, if people like what you are doing and think it will sell, they start coming to you with commercial schemes for doing many things with your work which you had never thought of doing. *You*, perhaps, had been hoping for recognition from scholars and critics. But *they* want to recognize it by printing it on paper cups and underpants. You pause (briefly) before signing the lucrative contract, knowing that no Pulitzer Prize has yet been awarded for paper cups or underpants. But then, you reflect, the times may change. . .

(Still, I must confess a certain pride in being possibly the only serious author privileged to see his own peculiar thoughts appearing on a wide variety of licensed products from tote-bags to cocktail-napkins, and even being publicly paraded around in the form of T-shirts on other people's chests. In one of my fantasies, I go about with a notebook, studying the chests of attractive persons who are wearing Ashleigh Brilliant T-Shirts, and, when asked what I'm doing, I reply: "I'm just collecting my thoughts.")

Ashleigh Brilliant

I'LL LISTEN TO YOUR UNREASONABLE DEMANDS

IF YOU'LL CONSIDER MY UNACCEPTABLE OFFER.

Something else, however, somewhat less pleasant, also happens if what you are doing appears to be at all successful: other people start copying it, and you have to decide what to do about this. Of course, you could decide to ignore it, and altruistically donate your priceless creations to the public domain. But I decided from the beginning that that was not my game. In the game I was playing, each of my creations was my property, and I was entitled to be protected from theft. So I carefully copyrighted all my works, and, whenever a case of infringement came up, I immediately took whatever legal action was necessary to stop it, regardless of cost. These actions are always successful in the end, but some of the cases have been so unusual that they are making legal history. In one case, one of my *Thoughts* (it happens also to be the title of this book) appeared without my authorization on a T-shirt worn in a network television "Movie of the Week." The makers of the film (Universal City Studios) eventually acknowledged my copyright and paid for the right to use my twelve words (at a very high rate per word). In another, much more complicated, case, which involved hiring lawyers in three different countries, a large firm in Germany was forced to stop translating my cards into Dutch and selling them in Holland. Even mighty *Time* magazine, after hearing from my lawyer concerning one of my *Thoughts* which they had reproduced without my permission and without credit (*Time,* July 27, 1970, p.8), agreed to publish an acknowledgement of my authorship and copyright (Sept. 14, 1970, p. 8). These have all been milestones in the long process of securing legitimacy at the highest levels for my hitherto unheard-of species of literary art.

But what about Fame? Is not that, too, part of the game? Like many others before me, I have been afflicted with a vision of greatness and a desire to enjoy whatever good things this world may have to offer, combined with a feeling that all is vanity. If one must be a celebrity, however, it is consoling to be celebrated for something so relatively harmless as creating a new medium of communication. And I never tire totally of being told that something I have said has been found cheering, meaningful, and useful to somebody else. People who know my work do tend to behave towards me in a respectful and even admiring manner which somehow seems strangely inconsistent with the nature of the work itself, and makes me feel somewhat like the perpetrator of a successful hoax. But when I look about me at my fellow celebrities (most of whom have come to public attention through existing media, rather than by creating their own), I often feel that, by comparison, my own contribution to the general welfare has been a substantial one.

You Too Can Play

One other fascinating result of this large-scale experiment in what is now called "consciousness-raising" has been the development of what may very well be one of the world's oddest mail-order businesses. Every single one of my messages is kept permanently in print on postcards which can be ordered by mail from my own company. This enables anybody anywhere in the world to choose at leisure from a vast range of messages, finding just the right ones for their own particular needs; and it enables me to have a direct type of contact with my public which few other writers enjoy.

If you would like to play this part of the game, please send for my catalogue, which lists all the cards, including many hundreds not in this book, and help spread the happy habit of using them for personal, business, and official purposes. The price of the catalogue, which comes with sample cards and a beautiful order form, is currently (1979) one U.S. dollar. Please enclose that amount, or its equivalent in your own time and currency. My address is:

Ashleigh Brilliant
117 W. Valerio Street,
Santa Barbara, California 93101, U.S.A.

Communication

Even in the long unhappy years before there were *Brilliant Thoughts,* postcards (which have been in existence since the 1860's) attempted with both printed words and (more especially) with printed pictures, to help people communicate with each other. The subject of communication itself, however, was rarely dealt with. As you will see in this section, I have attempted to remedy this deficiency.

But isn't there something ominous about the growing use of pre-fabricated messages? My post cards provide the senders with plenty of space to add their own personal messages—but what sort of things are they saying? It happens that Fate and the Post Office have provided me with an excellent way of finding out. Any undeliverable first-class mail is always returned by the Post Office to the sender. But frequently people who send one of my cards neglect to put a return address on it. If it proves undeliverable for any reason, then it gets returned to *me*, since my own name and address happen to be printed on it. Thus I now have quite a large collection of these "used" *Brilliant Thoughts.* One thing they reveal is that many of my messages apparently do the job so well that often the only comment added by the sender is something like "How true" or "Need I say more?"

So I'm helping people to communicate, but am I not also helping them to become more and more inarticulate? Sometimes I play with the idea that all human thoughts and feelings could be computerized, and, given any particular situation, the machine could in a flash present you with exactly the right thing to say. This of course immediately conjures up the image of another computer ready to receive the message and instantaneously produce the correct reply.

On the more positive side, however, I do feel that the idea of making available very small pieces of thought, feelings (and why not many other types of information?) in a handy convenient format which (unlike a book) is very easily carried on the person, posted on a wall, or sent in the mail, may actually be an extremely useful and effective way of humanizing the computeristic trend towards an ultimate total codification of the human mind. Perhaps not only our machines but we ourselves could make somewhat more sense of the universe if it were broken up into little uniform pieces for us all to play with.

COMMUNICATE!

IT CAN'T
MAKE THINGS
ANY WORSE.

I DON'T WISH TO APPEAR
OVERLY INQUISITIVE,
BUT ARE YOU STILL ALIVE?

Ashleigh
Brilliant

POT-SHOTS NO. 281.

AGREE WITH ME NOW:

Ashleigh
Brilliant

IT WILL SAVE SO MUCH TIME.

20

POT-SHOTS NO. 1078.

YES, BUT EVERY TIME I TRY TO SEE THINGS YOUR WAY,

I GET A HEADACHE.

Ashleigh Brilliant

POT-SHOTS NO. 734.

WHAT GOOD IS IT IF I TALK IN FLOWERS

WHILE YOU'RE THINKING IN PASTRY?

Ashleigh Brilliant

When all other means of communication fail,

try words.

Ashleigh Brilliant

I WAITED AND WAITED,

AND WHEN NO MESSAGE CAME,

I KNEW IT MUST BE FROM YOU.

Ashleigh Brilliant

I WANT
TO REACH
YOUR MIND —

WHERE
IS IT
CURRENTLY
LOCATED?

Ashleigh
Brilliant

© BRILLIANT ENTERPRISES 1974

Ashleigh Brilliant POT-SHOTS NO. 1216.

WHEN I
SAY NOTHING,
I DON'T
NECESSARILY
MEAN
NOTHING.

© BRILLIANT ENTERPRISES 1977.

But there's nobody else around
for me to bore.

LET'S NOT COMPLICATE OUR RELATIONSHIP

BY TRYING TO COMMUNICATE WITH EACH OTHER.

Ashleigh
Brilliant

WORDS
CAN NEVER EXPRESS

**WHAT WORDS
CAN NEVER
EXPRESS.**

I'M WRITING
TO TELL YOU
I HAVE NOTHING TO SAY

Ashleigh
Brilliant

Ashleigh
Brilliant

INFORM ALL
THE TROOPS THAT
COMMUNICATIONS
HAVE
COMPLETELY
BROKEN
DOWN.

© BRILLIANT ENTERPRISES 1970

Ashleigh
Brilliant

I'LL PRETEND TO
TRUST YOU....

IF YOU'LL
PRETEND TO
TRUST ME.

People Are Like That

Human nature, like everything else, is changing. (In many ways, for example, we are much more kind, or at least less cruel, to people and creatures for whose feelings our ancestors had little regard). But here are some snapshots of it taken from a concealed position in the back of my own mind. I claim no special knowledge, other than perhaps an ability to savor the ridiculous. A drama critic might call my medium "The Postcard of the Absurd."

If you feel personally involved in many (or any) of these "snapshots," it is because I am like a good writer of horoscopes, whose art or contrivance it is to combine generalities and specifics in such a way that the reader can always find something to relate to. This (if you like) is a cheap trick, and it becomes cheaper (and more effective) the more I play it. The more different messages I put into circulation, the more chance there is that everybody will eventually be reached by, and pleased by, at least one.

But I don't want merely to amuse. Like every starry-eyed prophet, I want to help human nature keep changing and improving. And this series of little tricks is, I hope, one of the safer ways of doing it.

PLEASE DON'T PUT A STRAIN ON OUR FRIENDSHIP

BY
ASKING ME
TO DO SOMETHING
FOR YOU.

Ashleigh
Brilliant

ACCEPT ME
FOR WHAT I AM —

COMPLETELY
UNACCEPTABLE.

Ashleigh Brilliant

I HAVE JUST
DISCOVERED THE TRUTH,
AND CAN'T UNDERSTAND
WHY EVERYBODY
ISN'T EAGER
TO HEAR IT.

Ashleigh Brilliant

© BRILLIANT ENTERPRISES 1977.

© BRILLIANT ENTERPRISES 1977   POT-SHOTS NO. 1032.

PLEASE
REMAIN
CALM

Ashleigh Brilliant

IT'S
NO USE
BOTH OF US
BEING
HYSTERICAL
AT THE
SAME TIME.

POT-SHOTS NO. 405

To any
truly impartial person,
it would be
obvious that
I am always right.

Ashleigh Brilliant

© BRILLIANT ENTERPRISES 1973

29

YOU ARE DEFINITELY ON MY LIST

BUT I'VE FORGOTTEN WHAT IT'S A LIST OF.

Ashleigh Brilliant

30

All I ask
of Life
is a constant
and exaggerated
sense of
my own importance.

The help I need
most urgently

is help in admitting

that I need help.

I NEED
SOME OF MY PROBLEMS

TO HELP
TAKE MY MIND OFF
SOME OF THE OTHERS.

Ashleigh Brilliant

MY BEST CONSOLATION
IS THE HOPE

THAT THE THINGS
I FAILED TO GET

WERE'NT REALLY
WORTH HAVING.

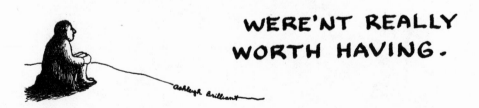

Ashleigh Brilliant

Ashleigh Brilliant

IF ONLY
I COULD GET
THAT WONDERFUL FEELING
OF ACCOMPLISHMENT

WITHOUT
HAVING TO
ACCOMPLISH
ANYTHING.

I CAN DO WITHOUT
THE ESSENTIALS,
BUT I MUST HAVE
MY LUXURIES.

Ashleigh
Brilliant

SAY SOMETHING
YOU'LL BE SORRY FOR—

I love
receiving
apologies.

THANK YOU
FOR LETTING ME
CRITICIZE YOU
SO UNFAIRLY:

Ashleigh
Brilliant

IT MAKES ME
FEEL
SO
IMPORTANT.

Ashleigh Brilliant

MY MIND IS OPEN

BY
APPOINTMENT
ONLY

THE TIME FOR ACTION IS PAST!

NOW IS THE TIME FOR SENSELESS BICKERING!

Ashleigh Brilliant

PLEASE FORGIVE ME IF, IN THE HEAT OF BATTLE,

I SOMETIMES FORGET WHICH SIDE I'M ON.

Ashleigh Brilliant

SOME OF THE THINGS
THAT WILL LIVE LONGEST
IN MY MEMORY

NEVER
REALLY
HAPPENED.

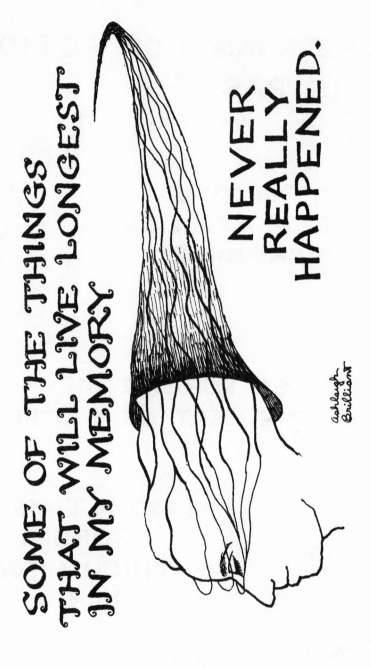

Ashleigh
Brilliant

I DEFINITELY INTEND
TO START LIVING
SOMETIME SOON.

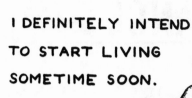

Ashleigh
Brilliant

Ashleigh
Brilliant

I resent
being treated

like the sort of person
I really
am.

I DESPERATELY
NEED SOME
WISE
ADVICE

WHICH WILL
RECOMMEND
THAT I DO
WHAT I
WANT TO DO.

Ashleigh
Brilliant

IT'S TIME FOR US
TO MAKE SOME BIG CHANGES —

WHY DON'T YOU CHANGE FIRST?

Ashleigh Brilliant

POT-SHOTS NO. 774.

Ashleigh Brilliant

I CAN ADMIT TO MYSELF THAT I WAS WRONG,

BUT I'LL NEVER ADMIT IT TO YOU.

EVERYBODY IS ENTITLED TO MY OPINION.

BEEN THROUGH HELL?

AND WHAT DID YOU BRING BACK FOR ME?

YOU ARE ALWAYS WELCOME IN MY TERRITORY

AT YOUR OWN RISK.

SEEING IS BELIEVING —

I WOULDN'T
HAVE SEEN IT
IF I HADN'T
BELIEVED IT.

Ashleigh
Brilliant

© BRILLIANT ENTERPRISES 1977.

© BRILLIANT ENTERPRISES 1972

POT-SHOTS NO. 331

Ashleigh
Brilliant

MY OPINIONS
MAY HAVE
CHANGED...

...BUT NOT
THE FACT
THAT I
AM RIGHT.

I ONLY OPENED

TO TELL YOU I'M CLOSED.

Ashleigh Brilliant

PLEASE RECONSIDER —
IT'S SO HARD
TO TAKE "GO TO HELL"
FOR AN ANSWER.

Ashleigh Brilliant

POT-SHOTS NO. 871

Ashleigh
Brilliant

HOW MUCH OF YOUR INFLUENCE ON ME

IS A RESULT OF MY INFLUENCE ON YOU?

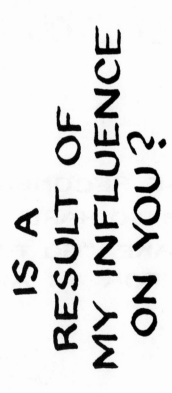

You And Me
Person-To-Person Messages

The basic message situation is that of one mind speaking to another. But every mind is full of contradictory thoughts and feelings. The most effective brief cries therefore (as seen on the following pages), tend to be those which give voice to internal conflicts. It is the starkness of juxtaposed opposites that creates in the recipient mind a sense of "true-ness," combined with a feeling of "funny-ness" which softens the hard edges of the truth.

The usefulness of such messages often lies in their ability to ease the awkwardness of difficult situations. For example, many types of business (and other) negotiations begin with a certain wariness, and even hostility, between the two sides. The atmosphere can be considerably lightened if somebody has the courage to say, "I'll listen to your unreasonable demands if you'll consider my unacceptable offer."

A sense of having something in common, even if it's something silly, is perhaps the most healthy and beneficial of all human emotional states.

I like to think of you

On days that begin
With a morning.

If you notice
that I'm deceiving you,
I can't be deceiving you
very well.

Ashleigh Brilliant

Ashleigh
Brilliant

If I didn't
understand you
so well,

I wouldn't
disagree
with you
so much.

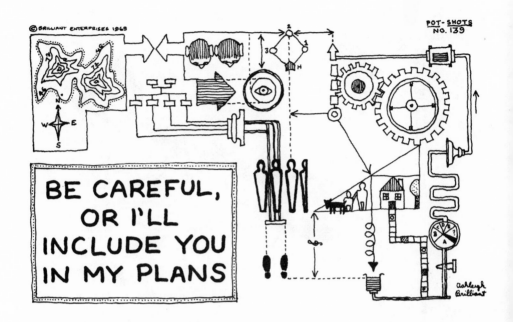

BE CAREFUL,
OR I'LL
INCLUDE YOU
IN MY PLANS

IF YOU DON'T LET ME
MAKE YOU HAPPY,
I'LL MAKE YOU SUFFER

Ashleigh
Brilliant

POT-SHOTS NO. 382

Ashleigh Brilliant

IF ONLY
I KNEW
YOU LOVED ME,

I COULD FACE
THE UNCERTAINTY

OF WHETHER
I LOVE YOU.

46

WHY IS IT
TAKING SO LONG
FOR YOU TO
BRING OUT
ALL THE
GOOD IN ME?

Ashleigh
Brilliant

YOU HAVE YOU
ON YOUR SIDE
BUT ALL I HAVE ON MY SIDE
IS ME

Ashleigh
Brilliant

HOW MUCH
DO I LOVE YOU?

— LESS THAN
YOU'LL EVER KNOW.

Ashleigh
Brilliant

IF ONLY
YOU WERE HERE
TO UPSET ME!

POT-SHOTS NO. 119

Ashleigh
Brilliant

WOULD YOU CARE
TO DRIFT AIMLESSLY
IN MY DIRECTION?

POT-SHOTS NO. 88

WE OUGHT TO BE MORE CAREFUL —

OUR LOVE COULD DRAG ON
FOR YEARS AND YEARS

Ashleigh Brilliant
©BRILLIANT ENTERPRISES 1968

Please don't lie to me,
unless you're
absolutely sure
I'll never
find out the truth.

Ashleigh Brilliant

POT-SHOTS NO. 590.

Ashleigh
Brilliant

I CAN FORGIVE YOU FOR BEING WRONG,

BUT IT'S MUCH HARDER

TO FORGIVE YOU FOR BEING RIGHT.

How kind of you
to want to live
my life for me.

Ashleigh Brilliant

WHAT SHALL
I DO
UNTIL YOU
IMPROVE?

Ashleigh Brilliant

Ashleigh Brilliant

PLEASE DON'T
RECOMMEND ME
TO YOUR FRIENDS —

IT'S DIFFICULT ENOUGH
TO COPE WITH
YOU ALONE.

IF THINGS DON'T IMPROVE SOON I MAY HAVE TO ASK YOU TO STOP HELPING ME

Ashleigh Brilliant

FORGIVE ME NOW

tomorrow I may
no longer
feel guilty

Ashleigh Brilliant

REMEMBER ME?

I'M THE
ONE WHO
NEVER MADE
ANY IMPRESSION ON YOU.

Ashleigh
Brilliant

POT-SHOTS
NO. 1286

YOU ARE NOT
THE ONLY PERSON
IN THE WORLD

WHO DOESN'T
CARE
ENOUGH
ABOUT ME.

Ashleigh
Brilliant

WHY ARE
YOU SO
HARD TO
IGNORE?

Ashleigh
Brilliant

POT-SHOTS NO.197.

IT WOULD BE NICE
TO SEE YOU AGAIN

AND AGAIN.

54

WE COULD
PROBABLY
BE FRIENDS

IF ONLY YOU
WOULD MAKE
THE FIRST
APPROACH.

Ashleigh Brilliant

Ashleigh Brilliant

HOW WOULD YOU LIKE TO BE

MY ULTIMATE DESTINATION?

POT-SHOTS NO. 211

Isn't it a nice
co-incidence

that you and I

are both alive
at the same time!

Ashleigh Brilliant

POT-SHOTS NO. 508

I'M VERY SENSITIVE
TO PLEASURE —

PLEASE DON'T
COME TOO
NEAR ME.

Ashleigh
Brilliant

POT-SHOTS NO. 40

YOU CAN PLAY WITH MY LIFE

IF YOU'LL LET ME PLAY WITH YOURS

Ashleigh
Brilliant

OUR LOVE IS GROWING

SO I
DON'T MIND

WATERING IT
OCCASIONALLY

WITH A FEW TEARS

Ashleigh Brilliant

Ashleigh Brilliant

DON'T EVER ASK ME

TO CHOOSE BETWEEN YOU AND HAPPINESS

BECAUSE I'D CHOOSE YOU EVERY TIME.

I DON'T
UNDERSTAND YOU

YOU DON'T
UNDERSTAND ME

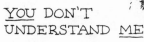

WHAT ELSE
DO WE HAVE
IN COMMON?

Ashleigh Brilliant

POT-SHOTS NO. 1222.

WHY ISN'T THERE
SOME CHEAP
AND EASY WAY
I CAN PROVE
HOW MUCH
YOU MEAN TO ME?

Ashleigh Brilliant

POT-SHOTS NO. 539

IF YOU
CARED MORE
FOR MY FEELINGS,

YOU WOULDN'T BE

SO SUCCESSFUL.

Ashleigh Brilliant

POT-SHOTS NO. 135

PLEASE DON'T ASK ME
WHAT THE SCORE IS —

I'M NOT EVEN SURE
WHAT GAME WE'RE PLAYING.

Ashleigh Brilliant

WHATEVER HAPPENED
TO ALL THE FUN
WE WERE GOING TO
HAVE TOGETHER?

Ashleigh
Brilliant

LET'S STAY TOGETHER

AND DRAG
EACH OTHER
DOWN.

Ashleigh
Brilliant

NOW THAT YOU
MENTION IT,

I DO
REMEMBER
LOVING YOU.

Ashleigh
Brilliant

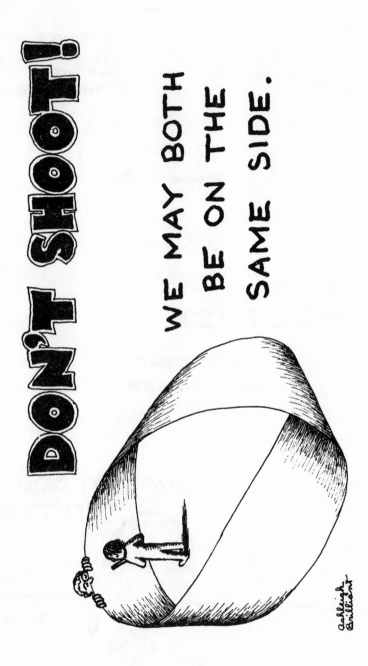

DON'T SHOOT!

WE MAY BOTH
BE ON THE
SAME SIDE.

Ashleigh
Brilliant

The Strange World of Other People

Somewhere out there, beyond good old You and Me, are the Others, who sometimes call themselves Society. They refuse, on the one hand, to leave us completely alone; or, on the other, to be as concerned as we are about the really important things. Society has some very odd ideas about how we should behave, and at times appears to be controlled by a vast system of inter-connecting stupidities.

But it is also Society, bless it, who buys my postcards, and is thus at least gradually in the process of re-educating itself. I always take it as a pat on the back whenever (as often happens) I walk into some strange office in a strange city, and see the desk of some harassed worker decorated with one of my inspiring cards, perhaps the one which says, "If we all work together, we can totally disrupt the system."

POT-SHOTS NO. 1280.

I WISH ALL THE PEOPLE
WHO SINCERELY WANT
TO HELP ME
COULD AGREE WITH EACH OTHER.

Ashleigh Brilliant

POT-SHOTS NO. 247   ©BRILLIANT ENTERPRISES 1971

PLEASE DON'T ASK ME

TO KEEP IN STEP —

Ashleigh
Brilliant

IT'S HARD ENOUGH

JUST TO STAY IN LINE.

I GET ALONG VERY WELL WITH EVERYBODY,

EXCEPT ANIMALS AND PEOPLE.

IN AN ORDERLY WORLD,

THERE'S ALWAYS A PLACE FOR THE DISORDERLY.

Ashleigh Brilliant

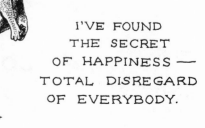

I'VE FOUND THE SECRET OF HAPPINESS — TOTAL DISREGARD OF EVERYBODY.

Ashleigh
Brilliant

POT-SHOTS NO. 363   ©BRILLIANT ENTERPRISES 1972

I WISH
I'D BEEN BORN WITH
AN UNFAIR ADVANTAGE,

INSTEAD OF HAVING TO
TRY TO ACQUIRE ONE.

©BRILLIANT ENTERPRISES 1974. POT-SHOTS NO. 614.

I HAD A TICKET
TO THE GOOD LIFE,

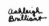

BUT SOMEHOW
COULD NEVER FIND
THE ENTRANCE.

I LIVE
IN A WORLD
OF MY OWN,

BUT VISITORS
ARE ALWAYS
WELCOME.

Ashleigh
Brilliant

WHAT I WANT IS
ALL THE
POWER
AND NONE
OF THE
RESPONSIBILITY.

Ashleigh Brilliant

I WANT
EITHER
LESS
CORRUPTION,

OR MORE
CHANCE
TO
PARTICIPATE
IN IT.

POT-SHOTS NO. 784.

SHOULD I
ABIDE BY
THE RULES
UNTIL THEY'RE
CHANGED,

OR HELP SPEED THE CHANGE
BY BREAKING THEM?

© BRILLIANT ENTERPRISES 1975.

Ashleigh Brilliant

67

FOR GOD'S SAKE
TELL ME WHAT TO THINK!

*Ashleigh
Brilliant*

THE WORLD NEEDS
MORE PEOPLE LIKE US
AND FEWER LIKE THEM.

Ashleigh Brilliant

GOOD LEADERS
ARE SCARCE,

*Ashleigh
Brilliant*

SO I'M
FOLLOWING
MYSELF.

LET'S ORGANIZE THIS THING

Ashleigh Brilliant

AND TAKE ALL THE FUN OUT OF IT.

IT MAY OR MAY NOT BE WORTHWHILE, BUT IT STILL HAS TO BE DONE.

Ashleigh Brilliant

POT-SHOTS NO. 1328.

THE MORE
WE DISAGREE,
THE MORE CHANCE THERE IS
THAT AT LEAST ONE OF US
IS RIGHT

Ashleigh Brilliant

© BRILLIANT ENTERPRISES 1977.

I DON'T CARE
WHAT THE WORLD
KNOWS
ABOUT ME

BUT I HOPE
MY MOTHER
NEVER
FINDS OUT.

Ashleigh Brilliant

I'M TOO BUSY
TO HAVE TIME FOR
ANYTHING
IMPORTANT.

Ashleigh Brilliant

NO MAN IS AN ISLAND

Ashleigh Brilliant

BUT SOME OF US ARE LONG PENINSULAS.

IT'S INTERESTING
TO KNOW THAT
MANY DISTINGUISHED PEOPLE
HAVE BODIES
VERY SIMILAR
TO MINE.

Ashleigh Brilliant

IF I DIDN'T HAVE MOST OF MY FRIENDS,

I WOULDN'T HAVE MOST OF MY PROBLEMS.

Ashleigh
Brilliant

THANK YOU FOR NOT ANNOYING ME ANY MORE THAN YOU DO.

Ashleigh
Brilliant

IT WAS ALL SO DIFFERENT BEFORE EVERYTHING CHANGED.

Time and Change

As we all know, change is definitely not what it used to be; but it is still rather mysterious and so, also, despite many improvements in clocks and watches, is the thing we call time. Of course, we all have a certain kind of inside information on these matters, and in many ways we know more than we think we do. We know, for example, how to travel into the future. What we don't know is how to go the other way, or how to go at any other speed than sixty minutes per hour.

But at least we are all in this together, and, as any writer of *Brilliant Thoughts* will tell you, the subject is one which everybody seems to respond to, even though the mood of the message may be quite a sad one. It's surprising how poignant a feeling can be conveyed in a very few words, when the subject is one on which both writer and reader are already well in tune. Actually, I never realized the true power of words until I began to limit my published utterances to seventeen of them.

The trouble is that words change like everything else, and sometimes come to mean exactly the opposite of what they once meant. ("Don't let me" meant "Don't hinder me" in Shakespeare's time.) I can only hope that they won't have changed too much more between the time of my transmission and your reception.

Everything might be different in the present,

Ashleigh Brilliant

if only one thing had been different in the past.

TODAY IS WHAT HAPPENED TO YESTERDAY.

Ashleigh Brilliant

NORMAL TIMES
MAY POSSIBLY BE
OVER FOREVER !

Ashleigh
Brilliant

SOME PARTS OF THE PAST
MUST BE PRESERVED,

Ashleigh
Brilliant

AND SOME OF
THE FUTURE
PREVENTED AT ALL COSTS.

MY GREAT AMBITION
IS
TO BUILD
SOMETHING
THAT WILL LAST,

Ashleigh
Brilliant

AT LEAST UNTIL
I'VE FINISHED
BUILDING IT.

TOMORROW, THIS WILL BE PART OF THE UNCHANGEABLE PAST

BUT FORTUNATELY, IT CAN STILL BE CHANGED TODAY.

LOOK! BEFORE OUR VERY EYES,

THE FUTURE IS BECOMING THE PAST.

SOME CHANGES ARE SO SLOW, YOU DON'T NOTICE THEM

OTHERS ARE SO FAST, THEY DON'T NOTICE YOU.

BEFORE I KNEW
THE BEST PART
OF MY LIFE
HAD COME,

*Ashleigh
Brilliant*

IT HAD GONE.

*Time
will end
all my
troubles,*

*Ashleigh
Brilliant*

*but I don't
always
approve of
Time's
methods.*

WHO WILL TAKE CARE OF THE WORLD
AFTER I'M GONE?

*Ashleigh
Brilliant*

THAN A CAUSE OF THE FUTURE.

I FIND IT EASIER TO BE A RESULT OF THE PAST

Ashleigh Brilliant

Ashleigh Brilliant

I NEED MORE TIME

AND I PROBABLY ALWAYS WILL.

WHY DOES TROUBLE ALWAYS COME AT THE WRONG TIME?

Ashleigh Brilliant

Until recently,
I thought I was
someone I knew.

Ashleigh
Brilliant

NOTHING IS
MORE QUIET
THAN THE SOUND
OF HAIR GOING GREY.

Ashleigh Brilliant

MY, HOW YOU'VE CHANGED

SINCE I'VE CHANGED.

Ashleigh
Brilliant

PLEASE
DON'T
DISTURB
ME

WHILE
I'M
GROWING.

Ashleigh
Brilliant

WASTING TIME

Ashleigh
Brilliant

IS AN IMPORTANT PART
OF LIVING.

WHERE WILL IT ALL END?

— PROBABLY SOMEWHERE NEAR WHERE IT ALL BEGAN.

Ashleigh Brilliant

84

The World, and Other Illusions

Returning to what we call consciousness, we always ask first, "Where am I?" Everything that happens, happens somewhere. So it is only natural for some big thoughts on small postcards to be concerned with places real and unreal, and the problem of which is which. As you will see, I do occasionally think about the World (although the World is famous for refusing to think very much about me), and have even gone out now and then to look at it, sometimes by hitch-hiking. I discovered that you could always get rides more easily if you carried a sign showing your destination. Now my cards like those in this chapter, serve a similar function, helping people to realize that we are all going the same way.

POT-SHOTS NO. 942.

SOMEHOW IT SEEMS
THE WORLD IS HAVING
MORE EFFECT
ON ME

THAN I'M HAVING ON THE WORLD.

Ashleigh Brilliant

POT-SHOTS NO. 1249.

Ashleigh Brilliant

I FEEL
DISILLUSIONED~

DO YOU
HAVE ANY
GOOD NEW
ILLUSIONS?

I HAVE ABANDONED
MY SEARCH FOR TRUTH,

AND AM
NOW LOOKING

FOR A GOOD
FANTASY.

Ashleigh Brilliant

POT-SHOTS NO. 591
Ashleigh
Brilliant

EITHER THIS
LIFE I'M IN
IS VERY DREAM—LIKE,

OR THIS
DREAM I'M IN
IS VERY LIFE—LIKE.

POT-SHOTS NO. 348

Ashleigh Brilliant

BE
REALISTIC,

AND ACCEPT
THE FACT

THAT
I LIVE...

...IN A
DREAM-WORLD.

© BRILLIANT ENTERPRISES 1972

POT-SHOTS NO. 570
Ashleigh
Brilliant

WHERE DO I GO,

NOW THAT I'VE
REACHED
MY LIMITS?

IT'S REALLY QUITE A SIMPLE CHOICE:

LIFE, DEATH, OR LOS ANGELES.

POT-SHOTS © BRILLIANT ENTERPRISES 1968
NO. 79

ashleigh Brilliant

I LIKE TO TRAVEL —

IT MAKES
ME FEEL
I'M GETTING SOMEWHERE.

© BRILLIANT ENTERPRISES 1971

Ashleigh Brilliant

© BRILLIANT ENTERPRISES 1971

POT-SHOTS No. 278

DUE TO CIRCUMSTANCES
BEYOND MY CONTROL,
I AM MASTER OF MY FATE
AND CAPTAIN OF MY SOUL.

Ashleigh Brilliant

© BRILLIANT ENTERPRISES 1975.

POT-SHOTS No. 830

Ashleigh Brilliant

LIVING ON EARTH
MAY BE EXPENSIVE,

BUT IT INCLUDES
AN ANNUAL FREE TRIP
AROUND THE SUN.

I DON'T GREATLY NEED
THE OUTSIDE WORLD,

but I do
like to know
that it's
still there.

ashleigh
Brilliant

POT-SHOTS NO. 415

ARE YOU
ON MY SIDE...

OR THE
WORLD'S
SIDE?

ashleigh
Brilliant

POT-SHOTS NO. 189

PLEASE HELP KEEP
THE WORLD CLEAN:
OTHERS MAY WISH
TO USE IT.

ashleigh
Brilliant

IT'LL BE A
NICE WORLD
IF THEY EVER
GET IT FINISHED

KEEP UP THE GOOD WORK!

BUT PLEASE DON'T ASK ME TO HELP.

ALL THE EVIDENCE CONCERNING THE UNIVERSE HAS NOT YET BEEN COLLECTED,

 SO THERE'S STILL HOPE.

Ashleigh Brilliant

ACCORDING TO ALL THE LATEST REPORTS,

Ashleigh Brilliant

THERE WAS NO TRUTH IN ANY OF THE EARLIER REPORTS.

THERE'S ONLY ONE EVERYTHING.

Ashleigh Brilliant

EVERYTHING IS CONTROLLED BY A SMALL EVIL GROUP

TO WHICH, UNFORTUNATELY, NOBODY I KNOW BELONGS.

Ashleigh Brilliant

GETTING THERE IS ONLY HALF AS FAR

AS GETTING THERE AND BACK.

Ashleigh Brilliant

I'LL NEVER SEE
ALL THE PLACES,
OR READ
ALL THE BOOKS,

BUT
FORTUNATELY,

THEY'RE NOT ALL RECOMMENDED.

Ashleigh
Brilliant

© BRILLIANT ENTERPRISES 1977.

© BRILLIANT ENTERPRISES 1974.

Every time
I close the door on Reality,
it comes in
through the window.

Ashleigh
Brilliant

© BRILLIANT ENTERPRISES 1971 POT-SHOTS NO. 303

IF YOU
LIKED
THE
EARTH

YOU'LL
LOVE
HEAVEN

Ashleigh
Brilliant

IS THERE A LIFE
BEFORE BREAKFAST?

Ashleigh Brilliant

I'M LOOKING FOR
THE PERFECT PILLOW —

I THINK IT'S
SOMEWHERE
NEAR YOURS.

Ashleigh Brilliant

What Is Your Pleasure?

Strange as it seems, life can actually be enjoyable; and there are even some people who believe that the good parts are worth the bad parts. Be that as it may, no survey of the universe would be complete without at least some reference to the odd phenomenon of human pleasure. No doubt it will not be too much longer before medical science, which has done us so many other services, will enable us to stimulate directly and at will the pleasure-centers of the brain, thereby rendering completely obsolete all the old-fashioned pleasure-devices, contrivances, practices, and substances, all the things we had to do with and to our bodies in order to get fleeting feelings of enjoyment. Until that happy day, we must painfully extract whatever entertainment is available from food, sex, games, spectacles, and various other titillations, trying somehow to prove that pleasure can be fun.

ALL I ASK IS A CHANCE TO PROVE THAT

MONEY CAN'T MAKE ME HAPPY.

Ashleigh Brilliant

ONE OF MY FAVORITE WAYS TO END A GAME IS BY WINNING.

Ashleigh
Brilliant

IF YOU CAN'T LEARN TO DO IT WELL,

Ashleigh
Brilliant

LEARN TO ENJOY DOING IT BADLY.

THE KIND OF DANGER I MOST ENJOY

 IS THE KIND I CAN WATCH FROM A SAFE PLACE.

MY OBJECT IS TO SAVE THE WORLD,

WHILE STILL LEADING A PLEASANT LIFE.

THE SUREST WAY
TO REMAIN A WINNER
IS TO WIN ONCE,
AND THEN NOT PLAY ANY MORE.

© BRILLIANT ENTERPRISES 1974.

© BRILLIANT ENTERPRISES 1977   POT-SHOTS NO. 1268.

I WILL STOP
AT NOTHING
TO REACH MY
OBJECTIVE,

BUT ONLY BECAUSE
MY BRAKES
ARE DEFECTIVE.

Ashleigh Brilliant

© BRILLIANT ENTERPRISES 1969

WHEN ALL ELSE FAILS,

EAT!

POT-SHOTS NO. 142

ANYTHING IS GOOD IF IT'S MADE OF CHOCOLATE

Ashleigh
Brilliant

I DON'T NEED
A GREAT DEAL OF LOVE
BUT I DO NEED
A STEADY SUPPLY.

Ashleigh
Brilliant

But after you have gone

I will still have

PEANUT BUTTER!

Ashleigh
Brilliant

HELP IMPROVE MY APPEARANCE —

I'M MUCH
BETTER - LOOKING
WHEN I'VE BEEN
HUGGED.

WHAT WOULD LIFE BE

WITHOUT ME?

Ashleigh Brilliant

ENJOY YOURSELF

WHILE YOU'RE
STILL OLD.

Ashleigh Brilliant

THERE HAS BEEN
AN ALARMING INCREASE

IN THE NUMBER
OF THINGS

I KNOW
NOTHING ABOUT.

Ashleigh Brilliant

A Thousand Thinks

Brilliant Thoughts, as a whole, express no particular philosophy or point of view, and are no more intended to than a window is meant to express an opinion about what you see through it. But each separate *Thought* does have something very definite to say, particularly those in this section, which are largely concerned with religion, philosophy, morality, and knowledge. Although it has been traditionally felt that such matters do not readily lend themselves to popular treatment, my experience indicates that the public is willing to give its total attention to any subject, no matter how profound, so long as you present it with wit, intelligence, and compassion, and discuss it fully from all sides in no more than seventeen words.

Ministers of various persuasions often write to tell me that they have used my *Thoughts* as texts for sermons. This conjures up pleasant fantasies about my works somehow becoming a new kind of Bible. Every great movement needs a Holy Book of some kind—could there be a "holy postcard"?

I NEVER GO ANYWHERE

WITHOUT
MY
SOUL.

Ashleigh
Brilliant

©BRILLIANT ENTERPRISES 1974

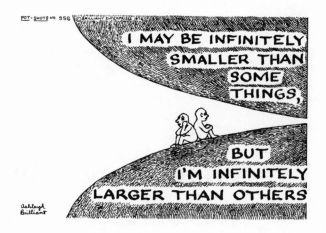

I MAY BE INFINITELY SMALLER THAN SOME THINGS,

BUT I'M INFINITELY LARGER THAN OTHERS

Ashleigh
Brilliant

THERE'S NOTHING
VERY MYSTERIOUS
ABOUT ME,

EXCEPT THAT
NOBODY REALLY KNOWS

Ashleigh
Brilliant

MY ORIGIN, PURPOSE, OR DESTINATION.

What makes the Universe so hard to comprehend

is that
there's nothing
to
compare it with.

Ashleigh Brilliant

I don't have any solution,
but I
certainly
admire
the problem.

Ashleigh Brilliant

POT-SHOTS NO. 1347.

© BRILLIANT ENTERPRISES 1977.

Ashleigh Brilliant

LIFE MAY HAVE NO MEANING

OR, EVEN WORSE,

IT MAY HAVE A MEANING OF WHICH I DISAPPROVE.

POT-SHOTS NO. 930

Ashleigh
Brilliant

I HAVE
A THEORY
THAT IT'S
IMPOSSIBLE
TO PROVE
ANYTHING,

BUT
I CAN'T
PROVE IT.

© BRILLIANT ENTERPRISES 1976

POT-SHOTS NO. 717

Ashleigh
Brilliant

SCIENCE
MAY
SOMEDAY
DISCOVER

WHAT FAITH
HAS ALWAYS
KNOWN.

© BRILLIANT ENTERPRISES 1975.

It's possible that my whole purpose in life is simply to serve as a warning to others.

Ashleigh Brilliant

Ashleigh Brilliant

SURELY
I DESERVE
SOME KIND OF
RECOGNITION

FOR ALL THE
BAD THINGS
I HAVEN'T DONE.

THIS LIFE IS MINE

Ashleigh Brilliant

SOME OF IT
WAS GIVEN TO ME;

THE REST, I MADE MYSELF.

I'M JUST
MOVING CLOUDS
TODAY—

TOMORROW
I'LL TRY
MOUNTAINS.

Ashleigh Brilliant

POT-SHOTS NO. 567

© BRILLIANT ENTERPRISES 1974.

IF ONLY I HAD FEWER NEEDS,

AND YOU HAD MORE ABILITY

TO SATISFY THEM!

Ashleigh
Brilliant

I am currently
going through
a difficult transition period
called "Life."

Ashleigh
Brilliant

OF COURSE I HAVE A PURPOSE --
TO FIND A PURPOSE.

Ashleigh
Brilliant

POT-SHOTS NO 24

BRING ME A DICTIONARY:

I WANT
TO KNOW
THE MEANING
OF LIFE.

Ashleigh Brilliant

EDUCATION

HAS SO MUCH TO LEARN!

Ashleigh
Brilliant

SCHOOL IS BAD ENOUGH—
BUT AT LEAST
I'M NOT LETTING THEM
TEACH ME ANYTHING.

Ashleigh
Brilliant

IF YOU LEARN ONE USELESS THING EVERY DAY, IN A SINGLE YEAR YOU'LL LEARN 365 USELESS THINGS.

Ashleigh Brilliant

YOUR REASONING
IS EXCELLENT —

Ashleigh
Brilliant

$$1 = 3$$
$$\therefore 4 = 6$$
$$\therefore 4 + 4 = 10$$
$$\therefore 2 + 2 = 5 \,!$$

IT'S ONLY
YOUR BASIC
ASSUMPTIONS
THAT ARE WRONG.

WHATEVER
BECAME OF
ETERNAL
TRUTH ?

Ashleigh
Brilliant

HOW TIRED I FEEL!

I UNDERSTOOD
SO MUCH
TODAY.

Ashleigh
Brilliant

POT-SHOTS NO. 937.

FUNDAMENTALLY,
THERE MAY BE
NO BASIS
FOR
ANYTHING.

Ashleigh
Brilliant

POT-SHOTS NO. 391

Ashleigh
Brilliant

THINKING ABOUT IT
IS EASIER THAN DOING IT —

BUT SO FAR,
I HAVEN'T EVEN
THOUGHT ABOUT IT.

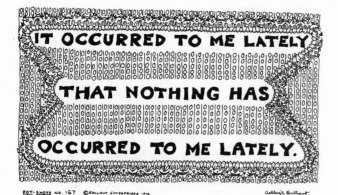

IT OCCURRED TO ME LATELY

THAT NOTHING HAS

OCCURRED TO ME LATELY.

POT-SHOTS NO. 167 © BRILLIANT ENTERPRISES 1976   *Ashleigh Brilliant*

Ashleigh Brilliant

IF LIFE IS MERELY A JOKE,

THE QUESTION STILL REMAINS:

FOR WHOSE AMUSEMENT?

HISTORY IS ON OUR SIDE

Ashleigh Brilliant

as long as we can control the historians.

LIFE CAN BE SO TRAGIC —

YOU'RE HERE TODAY

AND HERE TOMORROW

118

Life and Other Problems

Let us be honest with ourselves: life is something which is here to stay—at least, as long as *we* are. It involves us totally—days, nights, and sometimes even weekends. It is no respecter of age or gender or social position, and even animals are said to have it.

What to do about it? Modern research suggests that it is all in the mind, and can be kept entirely under control with an occasional shock treatment. Rising to this occasion, I have devised many of the *Brilliant Thoughts* in this section to administer the necessary psychic jolts. Call it, if you will, in the great tradition of the "dirty postcard," a kind of philosophical pornography. Unfortunately, my statements are not always given credit for being as outrageous as they truly are. Upton Sinclair said of his novel *The Jungle* that he aimed at the public's heart and hit its stomach. Sometimes I feel I have aimed at the public's brain, and merely hit its funny-bone.

I'M SECRETLY
VERY INTERESTED
IN LIFE.

<u>POT-SHOTS</u> NO. 103

Ashleigh
Brilliant

<u>POT-SHOTS</u> NO. 420

MY PICTURE
OF THE WORLD
KEEPS CHANGING
BEFORE I CAN
GET IT INTO FOCUS.

Ashleigh
Brilliant

IF YOU'RE CAREFUL ENOUGH, NOTHING BAD OR GOOD WILL EVER HAPPEN TO YOU.

Ashleigh
Brilliant

CHEER UP!

THINGS MAY BE GETTING WORSE AT A SLOWER RATE.

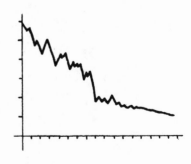

Ashleigh Brilliant

© BRILLIANT ENTERPRISES 1971

MAYBE I'M LUCKY
TO BE GOING
SO SLOWLY

BECAUSE
I MAY BE GOING
IN THE WRONG DIRECTION

Ashleigh Brilliant

BY DOING
JUST A LITTLE
EVERY DAY,

Ashleigh Brilliant

I CAN
GRADUALLY
LET THE TASK
COMPLETELY
OVERWHELM ME.

© BRILLIANT ENTERPRISES 1977.

Ashleigh Brilliant

IF I DON'T DO
THE THINGS
THAT ARE NOT
WORTH DOING,
WHO WILL?

© BRILLIANT ENTERPRISES 1974

I MEANT
NO HARM BY
STAYING ALIVE!
I ONLY DID IT
FOR A JOKE!

POT-SHOTS NO. 485
© BRILLIANT ENTERPRISES 1974

NO USE GETTING
TOO INVOLVED IN LIFE
— I'M ONLY HERE FOR
A LIMITED TIME.

© BRILLIANT ENTERPRISES 1870   POT-SHOTS NO. 151

I THINK I'LL JUST SIT HERE

AND WAIT TILL LIFE GETS EASIER

OH WELL,
I GUESS THIS IS JUST
GOING TO BE
ONE OF THOSE LIFETIMES!

NO, LIFE ISN'T WHAT I WANTED --

HAVEN'T YOU GOT ANYTHING ELSE?

I AM FIGHTING FOR SURVIVAL

in my own
sweet and
gentle way.

Ashleigh Brilliant

SOMETIMES I GET
AN ALMOST IRRESISTIBLE URGE
TO GO ON LIVING

Ashleigh Brilliant

I'M TRYING TO LIVE MY LIFE —

A TASK SO DIFFICULT,
IT HAS NEVER BEEN
ATTEMPTED BEFORE.

SOMEDAY I'LL GET MY BIG CHANCE—

OR HAVE I ALREADY HAD IT?

Ashleigh Brilliant

ALL I WANT IS A LITTLE MORE THAN I'LL EVER GET.

Ashleigh Brilliant

I FEEL MUCH BETTER, NOW THAT I'VE GIVEN UP HOPE.

Ashleigh Brilliant

129

ONE POSSIBLE REASON
WHY THINGS
AREN'T GOING
ACCORDING
TO PLAN

IS THAT
THERE NEVER
WAS A PLAN.

© BRILLIANT ENTERPRISES 1974

© BRILLIANT ENTERPRISES 1976.

I HOPE
THE LIFE-INSPECTOR
DOESN'T
COME AROUND
WHILE
I HAVE
MY LIFE
IN SUCH A MESS.

Ashleigh Brilliant

I HOPE I GET WHAT I WANT

Ashleigh
Brilliant

Before I stop wanting it.

I'M DOING MY PART TO HELP PRESERVE LIFE ON EARTH

Ashleigh
Brilliant

BY TRYING TO PRESERVE MY OWN.

I RECENTLY
HAD MY PROBLEMS
ON THE RUN,

BUT NOW
THEY'VE
RE-GROUPED,
AND ARE
MAKING
ANOTHER
ATTACK.

Ashleigh Brilliant

It takes
a special kind
of courage

to face
what we all have to face.

Ashleigh Brilliant

Ashleigh Brilliant

TO BE SURE
OF HITTING
THE TARGET,

SHOOT FIRST

AND, WHATEVER YOU HIT,
CALL IT THE TARGET.

I'M GROWING OUT OF
SOME OF MY PROBLEMS,

BUT
THERE ARE OTHERS
I'M GROWING INTO.

© BRILLIANT ENTERPRISES 1977.

© BRILLIANT ENTERPRISES 1977.

POT-SHOTS NO. 1044.

BY TRYING
VERY HARD
TO
IMPROVE
THINGS,

I AM
OFTEN ABLE
TO MAKE THEM
MUCH WORSE.

© BRILLIANT ENTERPRISES 1972

POT-SHOTS NO. 312

IF YOU DON'T DO IT,

YOU'LL NEVER KNOW

WHAT WOULD HAVE HAPPENED

IF YOU HAD DONE IT.

POT-SHOTS NO. 1146

I wish
I had done
some of the
hard things

when they were
easier to do.

Ashleigh
Brilliant

POT-SHOTS NO. 918.

Ashleigh
Brilliant

HOW CAN I
POSSIBLY
HAVE COME
SO FAR,

AND YET
STILL HAVE
SO FAR TO GO?

Ashleigh
Brilliant

EVERY SUCCESSFUL PERSON HAS HAD FAILURES

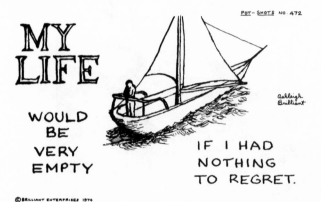

BUT
REPEATED FAILURE
IS NO GUARANTEE
OF
EVENTUAL SUCCESS.

MY LIFE

Ashleigh
Brilliant

WOULD
BE
VERY
EMPTY

IF I HAD
NOTHING
TO REGRET.

TRY TO HAVE AS GOOD A LIFE AS YOU CAN, UNDER THE CIRCUMSTANCES.

© BRILLIANT ENTERPRISES 1974

IT'S ONLY
MY TENSION
THAT'S
HOLDING ME
TOGETHER.

PLEASE
DON'T
TELL ME
TO RELAX—

Ashleigh
Brilliant

Health, Death, and Other Mysterious Conditions

Who or what is healthy? It's getting harder and harder to tell. And the latest uncertainty being inflicted on us by Science is that we are no longer sure when we are dead. It used to be that the only forms of literature which discussed these matters were heavy books and even heavier tombstones. My postcards provide a lighter forum. Nowadays people actually write to ask if they may quote a *Brilliant Thought* on their own tombstone. I grant permission, on condition that they also include on the stone a correct copyright notice. (Thus one of my fantasies has been fulfilled—to write words so meaningful that people would want to carve them in stone. Another fantasy has been to become required reading in schools and colleges. This too has been fulfilled, in the form of many requests to be quoted and reproduced in text-books.)

One group to whom these particular messages seem to have special appeal are those who call themselves "Immortalists"—people who believe that what we call "death" may be only some kind of disease for which we haven't yet developed a cure. I sincerely wish them and their movement good health and long life.

I WISH I HAD MORE ENERGY...

...OR LESS AMBITION.

Ashleigh Brilliant

FORCE YOURSELF TO RELAX

Ashleigh Brilliant

IT'S
VERY
INCONVENIENT
TO BE
MORTAL ~

Ashleigh Brilliant

YOU
NEVER KNOW
WHEN
EVERYTHING
MAY SUDDENLY
STOP HAPPENING.

© BRILLIANT ENTERPRISES 1976.

© BRILLIANT ENTERPRISES 1974.

Ashleigh Brilliant

IS DEATH
LEGALLY
BINDING?

POT-SHOTS NO. 1098.

WHAT SHOULD I DO
IF MY PROBLEMS
AREN'T ALL
SOLVED
BY THE TIME
I DIE?

© BRILLIANT ENTERPRISES 1977   Ashleigh Brilliant

POT-SHOTS NO. 1283.

TELL THE SCIENTISTS
TO HURRY———

I DON'T WANT TO DIE
BEFORE THEY DISCOVER
HOW TO SAVE ME.

Ashleigh
Brilliant

© BRILLIANT ENTERPRISES 1977.

© BRILLIANT ENTERPRISES 1974.

POT-SHOTS NO. 564
Ashleigh
Brilliant

I AM NOT DEAD YET

*but watch for
further reports.*

I could live
a better life,
if I had
a better mind
and a better body.

Ashleigh
Brilliant

Ashleigh
Brilliant

I'M DOING
WHAT I CAN
TO
PROLONG
MY LIFE,

HOPING THAT
SOMEDAY
I'LL LEARN
WHAT IT'S FOR.

POT-SHOTS NO. 1310.

WHAT CAUSES
THE MYSTERIOUS DEATH
OF
EVERYBODY?

Ashleigh Brilliant

POT-SHOTS NO. 588
Ashleigh Brilliant

I may be gone tomorrow,

but that won't mean

that I wasn't here today.

POT-SHOTS NO. 1124.

I WANT
ALL MY
POSTHUMOUS MEDALS
IN ADVANCE.

Ashleigh Brilliant

I NEED A GOOD
IMAGINARY CURE
FOR MY PAINFUL
IMAGINARY AILMENT.

HALF THE TIME
I'M TOO COLD,
AND HALF
TOO HOT ~

SO, AT LEAST
ON AVERAGE,
I'M COMFORTABLE.

ONE THING ABOUT PAIN:

IT PROVES

YOU'RE

ALIVE!

MY ARMS ARE ACHING TO HOLD YOU

OR IS IT
ARTHRITIS ?

Ashleigh Brilliant

SOMETIMES THE BEST MEDICINE IS TO STOP TAKING SOMETHING.

Ashleigh Brilliant

AT THE END
OF MY LIFE,
THERE'LL BE A GOOD REST,

AND NO FURTHER
ACTIVITIES
ARE SCHEDULED.

Ashleigh
Brilliant

© BRILLIANT ENTERPRISES 1977.

I HOPE
THE DAY AFTER I DIE
IS A NICE DAY.

Ashleigh
Brilliant

Ashleigh
Brilliant

IF I CAN
SURVIVE DEATH,
I CAN PROBABLY
SURVIVE
ANYTHING.

© BRILLIANT ENTERPRISES 1975.

YES, BUT
WHICH SELF
DO YOU WANT
ME TO BE?

Ashleigh
Brilliant

The Crowded Self

When my own strange thoughts began to be widely circulated as postcards, it pleased and surprised me to learn that many counsellors, psychiatrists, and others working in the field of Mental Health were finding them useful in their work, particularly (it seems) for stimulating their patients to think and talk about their own problems. This had never been any part of my original purpose—in fact, I was astonished. What had I done to become suddenly so useful to so many people? Nothing that many or most others couldn't do if they had thought of it. I had simply put many small pieces of myself on many small pieces of paper, and let them loose. They were about *my* problems, not yours. Suppose more people advertised their thoughts and feelings in this way! (Or in other ways!) Perhaps there wouldn't be so many mental health problems. (Or would there be *more*?)

One of the biggest of these problems apparently revolves around the question, "Who or what am I (or is me)?"

For some reason, this is a question rarely asked or discussed in the popular media. Yet our whole concept of "self" is currently undergoing drastic revision. We are no longer so sure as we once were that an "individual" is really in-dividual, that is, incapable of being divided. Blood transfusions, organ transplants, artificial body parts—and eventually, no doubt, the divided, transplanted, and re-arranged brain: perhaps these are all merely stages on the journey to a new Extended Self. In the hope that this may be so, I encourage you to consider that the self in the following messages may, at least occasionally, be yours.

THE PART OF THE WORLD WHICH I FIND MOST PUZZLING

IS THE PART CALLED "ME"

Ashleigh Brilliant

Ashleigh Brilliant

I'M LEARNING ABOUT PEOPLE THE HARD WAY—

BY BEING ONE.

THE ODDS ARE
A MILLION
TO ONE

AGAINST MY BEING
ONE IN A MILLION.

MY TRUE VALUE

DEPENDS ENTIRELY
ON
WHAT YOU
COMPARE
ME WITH.

Ashleigh
Brilliant

© BRILLIANT ENTERPRISES 1972

CONFIDENTIALLY,

I HAVE NOTHING WORTH HIDING.

Ashleigh Brilliant

I AM
UNCONDITIONALLY
GUARANTEED
TO BE
FULL OF DEFECTS.

Ashleigh Brilliant

IF YOU HAVE
DOUBTS ABOUT ME,
DON'T WORRY—

I HAVE MANY
ABOUT MYSELF.

*Ashleigh
Brilliant*

SOME
PARTS OF ME
ARE SO PRIVATE
THAT I MYSELF
HAVE
NO
KNOWLEDGE OF THEM.

Ashleigh Brilliant

WHEN YOU'RE BORN,
YOU'RE TAKING
A BIG CHANCE.

Ashleigh
Brilliant

BEWARE! I'M ACTING UNDER THE INFLUENCE OF HUMAN NATURE.

Ashleigh Brilliant

I'M READY TO GIVE UP THE STRUGGLE,

BUT CAN'T FIND ANYBODY TO SURRENDER TO.

Ashleigh Brilliant

IF YOU WANT TO PUT YOURSELF ON THE MAP,

PUBLISH YOUR OWN MAP.

Ashleigh Brilliant

SINGLE-HANDEDLY, I HAVE FOUGHT MY WAY INTO THIS HOPELESS MESS.

Ashleigh Brilliant

MOST OF MY FAULTS

Ashleigh Brilliant

ARE NOT MY FAULT.

I WISH THEY'D PASS MORE LAWS

TO PROTECT ME FROM MYSELF.

Ashleigh Brilliant

HELP! I'M TRAPPED IN A HUMAN BODY!

Ashleigh Brilliant

I'M IN SEARCH OF MYSELF —

HAVE YOU SEEN ME ANYWHERE?

Ashleigh Brilliant

IF I DON'T HAVE SOME INSANITY SOON, I'LL GO MAD!

Ashleigh Brilliant

If I go
out of my mind,
I'll do it quietly,
so as not to
disturb you.

Ashleigh Brilliant

DESPITE
ALL APPEARANCES,
I AM
A THINKING,
FEELING,
HUMAN BEING.

Ashleigh Brilliant

Ashleigh Brilliant

I HAD
SOME HAPPINESS
ONCE,

BUT WE
MOVED AWAY,

AND I HAD TO
LEAVE IT BEHIND.

If only
I could be
respected

Without having to be
respectable!

Ashleigh Brilliant

Ashleigh Brilliant

I WROTE MYSELF A THREATENING LETTER

AND RECEIVED A DEFIANT REPLY.

ONE OF THE WORST OF MY MANY FAULTS

IS THAT I'M TOO CRITICAL OF MYSELF.

Ashleigh Brilliant

New members are urgently needed in the Society for Prevention of Cruelty to Yourself.

Ashleigh Brilliant

Ashleigh
Brilliant

I WORK VERY HARD

PLEASE DON'T EXPECT ME TO THINK AS WELL.

Ashleigh
Brilliant

PLEASE DON'T SUPPLY ANY MORE INFORMATION

I'm already
Too well informed.

Ashleigh
Brilliant

IF I HAD BETTER TOOLS,

I COULD MORE EFFECTIVELY DEMONSTRATE

MY TOTAL INCOMPETENCE.

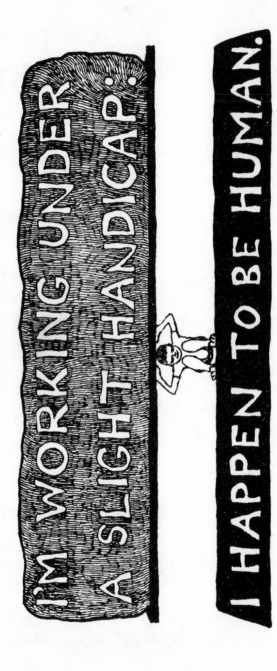

POT-SHOTS No. 429

© BRILLIANT ENTERPRISES 1973

I'M WORKING UNDER A SLIGHT HANDICAP:

I HAPPEN TO BE HUMAN.

Ashleigh Brilliant

160